STARRING

Flynn Rider

Rapunzel

Maximus

Stabbington brothers

Mother Gothel

First published by Parragon in 2010
Parragon
Chartist House
15-17 Trim Street
Bath BA1 1HA, UK
www.parragon.com

ISBN 978-1-4075-3679-8
Printed in China

Disney Tangled

Adapted by Lisa Marsoli
Illustrated by Jean-Paul Orpiñas, Studio IBOIX,
and the Disney Storybook Artists

Bath · New York · Singapore · Hong Kong · Cologne · Delhi · Melbourne

Once upon a time, in a land far away, a drop of sunlight fell to the ground. It grew into a magical golden flower that possessed healing powers. An old woman named Mother Gothel discovered the flower, and hoarded its power to preserve her youth and beauty.

As centuries passed, a glorious kingdom was built close to the cliff where the flower grew. When the beloved queen fell ill, the townspeople searched for the legendary flower, until at last they found it. The flower made the Queen well, and she soon gave birth to a beautiful baby girl. The King and Queen launched a lantern into the sky in celebration.

One night, the vengeful Mother Gothel slipped into the nursery,
where she discovered that the healing power of the flower had transferred
into the baby's golden hair! Mother Gothel cut off a lock – but the hair lost
its power and turned brown. Mother Gothel knew that if she wanted to
stay young, she had to keep the child with her always. She snatched the
princess and vanished to a place where no one could find them. The King
and Queen were heartbroken.

Each year on the Princess's birthday, the King and Queen released
lanterns into the night sky. They hoped their light would guide their
princess home.

Mother Gothel kept Rapunzel locked in a soaring tower and raised her as a daughter. Though the woman pretended to love Rapunzel, she only truly loved Rapunzel's golden hair.

Rapunzel was happy with the companionship of Mother Gothel and her friend Pascal, the chameleon. But she had one dream that she longed to make come true.

On the day before her eighteenth birthday, Rapunzel told Mother Gothel what it was. "I want to see the floating lights!" she said, revealing a painting she had made of them. "They appear every year on my birthday – only on my birthday. And I can't help but feel like they're meant for me!"

Mother Gothel told Rapunzel she was too weak and helpless to handle the outside world. "Don't ever ask to leave this tower again," she said.

Meanwhile, in another part of the forest, a thief named Flynn Rider was on the run with his partners in crime, the Stabbington brothers. Flynn clutched tightly to a satchel that held a stolen royal crown!

Flynn knew the Stabbingtons were too dangerous to be trusted, so he left them and took off with the satchel. But the Captain of the Guard and his horse Maximus were on his heels! The tricky thief knocked the Captain off Maximus and landed in the saddle himself.

Maximus spun in circles until he sunk his teeth into the satchel. As Flynn yanked the satchel free, it went flying into the air.

The satchel snagged on a tree that extended over a cliff. Flynn and Maximus both made their way out onto the tree trunk. But the tree broke, sending the thief and horse toppling into the canyon below.

When they landed, Flynn took off before Maximus could pick up his scent. The thief ducked into a cave. When he emerged from the other side, he saw something amazing: an enormous tower. It would make the perfect hiding place!

He climbed the tower and scrambled into the open window at the top. Finally, he breathed a sigh of relief. He was safe!

CLANG!

Suddenly, everything went black.

Rapunzel had been so startled by the intruder, she snuck up behind him and hit him with a frying pan! Flynn was the first man she had ever seen. He didn't look like the scary ruffians that Mother Gothel had warned her about. Rapunzel thought he was actually pleasant-looking.

After making sure he was unconscious, Rapunzel dragged Flynn to the closet and stuffed him inside. Rapunzel felt exhilarated! Surely this act of bravery would prove to Mother that she could handle herself in the outside world.

Then Rapunzel noticed the mysterious gold object in Flynn's satchel. She placed it on top of her head and gazed into the mirror. She felt different somehow.

Suddenly, Mother Gothel arrived. Rapunzel brought up the floating lights again. She was about to show Mother the stranger in the closet, but Mother cut her off.

"We're done talking about this. You are not leaving this tower! EVER!" roared Mother Gothel.

Ever? Rapunzel was shocked. Realizing she would never get out of the tower unless she took matters into her own hands, Rapunzel asked for another birthday present. She requested special paint that would require Mother to leave on a three-day journey.

Mother Gothel agreed to get the paint and left the tower. Not wasting another second, Rapunzel dragged Flynn out of the closet and offered him a deal. If Flynn took her to see the floating lights and returned her home safely, she would give him the satchel. Flynn had no choice but to agree.

As much as Rapunzel longed to leave the tower, when the moment came, she was terrified. She had never been outside before. But when she glanced back at her painting of the floating lights, Rapunzel overcame her fear and leaped!

With Pascal on her shoulder, she slid down her hair, stopping just inches above the ground. Slowly, Rapunzel touched one foot to the soft grass, then the other.

"I can't believe I did this! I can't believe I did this! I can't believe I did this!" she shouted as she rolled on the ground.

Rapunzel was having the time of her life, but she also felt like a terrible daughter for betraying Mother Gothel. One moment she was running gleefully through a meadow, the next she was sobbing facedown in a field of flowers.

Flynn tried to take advantage of Rapunzel's guilt by making her feel even worse. "Does your mother deserve this?" he asked. "No. Would it break her heart? Of course. I'm letting you out of the deal. Let's turn around and get you home."

Flynn's charms didn't work on Rapunzel.

"I'm seeing those lanterns," she insisted.

Not far from the tower, Mother Gothel came face to face with Maximus.

"A palace horse," she gasped, seeing the kingdom's sun symbol on Maximus' chest . She thought the guards had found Rapunzel. She turned and frantically raced back to the tower.

Mother Gothel searched everywhere, but Rapunzel was gone. Then she saw something shiny beneath the staircase. It was the crown in the satchel, along with Flynn's WANTED poster. Now she knew exactly who had taken Rapunzel – and nothing was going to stop her from finding him!

By this time, Flynn had led Rapunzel to a cosy-looking pub called the Snuggly Duckling. But inside, the place was filled with scary-looking thugs! Flynn was hoping to frighten Rapunzel into returning to the tower.

Then someone held up Flynn's WANTED poster. The pub thugs began fighting for the reward money – with Flynn caught right in the middle of the brawl.

Rapunzel banged her frying pan on a giant pot to get the thugs' attention. She asked them to let Flynn go so that she could make her dream come true. To Rapunzel's surprise, every one of the thugs had a secret dream, too.

Outside, Mother Gothel arrived at the pub. She looked into the window, and was shocked to see that Rapunzel had managed to befriend a room full of ruffians!

Suddenly, Maximus, the royal guards and the captive Stabbington brothers burst into the pub.

"Where's Rider?" demanded the Captain.

One of the thugs revealed a secret passageway to Flynn and Rapunzel. They gratefully disappeared into the dark tunnel.

Moments later, Maximus led the guards straight to the escape route. After they had left, the Stabbington brothers broke free and headed down the passageway themselves. They wanted the crown back!

Mother Gothel had seen everything, and made one of the thugs tell her where the tunnel ended.

Flynn and Rapunzel sprinted through the tunnel and skidded to the edge of an enormous cavern. Rapunzel lassoed her hair around a rock and jumped! She swung over the wide chasm and landed on a stone column. Meanwhile, Flynn fended off Maximus and the guards with Rapunzel's frying pan! Rapunzel tossed her hair to him and held on tight as Flynn swung through the air, right over the Stabbington brothers!

But they weren't safe yet. A dam suddenly burst, filling the entire cavern with water! Maximus, the guards and the Stabbingtons were washed away and Flynn and Rapunzel were trapped in a small cave.

The water quickly began to rise. As Flynn frantically searched for a way out, he cut his hand on the rocks.

"It's pitch black. I can't see anything," he said.

"This is all my fault," Rapunzel said tearfully. "I'm so sorry, Flynn."

"Eugene. My real name's Eugene Fitzherbert," Flynn admitted. "Someone might as well know."

Rapunzel revealed a secret of her own: "I have magic hair that glows when I sing."

Suddenly she realized her hair could light up the cave and show them the way out!

At the tunnel's exit, Mother Gothel waited for Flynn and Rapunzel, but the Stabbington brothers emerged instead. She offered them revenge on Flynn – and something even more valuable than the crown. The Stabbington brothers liked the sound of that!

Meanwhile, Rapunzel, Flynn and Pascal had made it safely to shore and built a campfire for the night. Rapunzel wrapped her hair around Flynn's injured hand and began to sing. Her glowing hair healed Flynn's wound. Flynn was dumbfounded.

He was finally beginning to understand how truly special Rapunzel was.

When Flynn went off to gather firewood, Mother Gothel appeared from the shadows of the woods to take Rapunzel back to the tower.

But Rapunzel refused to go back. "I met someone, and I think he likes me," she said.

Mother Gothel laughed at her. She handed Rapunzel the satchel with the crown and told her that it was all Flynn wanted. Once Rapunzel gave it to him, the thief would vanish. After Mother Gothel set the seeds of doubt, she retreated back into the forest. Rapunzel wanted to trust Flynn but she wasn't sure. She decided to hide the satchel in a nearby tree.

The next morning, Flynn woke up to Maximus trying to drag him away! Rapunzel came to Flynn's rescue and talked the horse into letting the thief go free for one more day.

As Flynn and Maximus shook on their truce, a bell rang in the distance. Rapunzel ran towards it until she came to the crest of a hill. Rapunzel gasped as the entire kingdom came into view. Her dream was just hours away from coming true!

Rapunzel, Flynn, Maximus and Pascal entered the gates of the kingdom. The town was the most exciting thing Rapunzel had ever experienced. A little boy greeted Rapunzel with a kingdom flag that had a golden sun symbol on it. Then a group of little girls braided Rapunzel's locks and pinned them up with flowers. Afterwards, Rapunzel and Flynn joined a crowd as a dance was about to begin.

Rapunzel was transfixed by a mosaic behind the stage. It was of
the King and Queen holding a baby girl with striking green eyes, just like
her own.

"Let the dance begin!" called an announcer.

Rapunzel and Flynn joined hands and began to whirl around the square.

After they danced, the couple visited shops and enjoyed the sights. All the while, they were getting to know each other better. It was a wonderful day!

As evening approached, Flynn led Rapunzel to a boat and rowed them to a spot with a perfect view of the kingdom.

As lanterns filled the sky, Rapunzel's heart soared. She gave Flynn the satchel, which she had kept hidden all day. She was no longer afraid he would leave her once he had the crown.

Beneath the glow of the lanterns, Rapunzel and Flynn held hands and gazed into each other's eyes.

Their romantic moment ended abruptly when Flynn spotted the Stabbington brothers watching them from the shore. Quickly, he rowed the boat to land.

"I'll be right back," he told Rapunzel as he grabbed the satchel and strode off.

Flynn gave the brothers the crown, but they wanted Rapunzel and her magic hair instead! He turned to go to Rapunzel, but the brothers knocked him unconscious, tied him to the helm of a boat and set him sailing into the harbour.

Then they came for Rapunzel. The brothers told her that Flynn had traded her for the crown. Rapunzel saw Flynn sailing away. She thought he had betrayed her!

Rapunzel ran off into the forest with the brothers in pursuit. Moments later, she heard Mother Gothel's voice. She ran back and found Mother standing over the unconscious Stabbingtons.

"You were right, Mother," said Rapunzel tearfully, hugging her tight.

Flynn's boat continued to sail until it crashed into a dock. Two guards found him tied up with the stolen crown and immediately dragged him off to prison.

Maximus was watching nearby. He had witnessed everything and knew he had to do something to save both Flynn and Rapunzel.

As Flynn was led down the prison corridors by the guards, he spotted the Stabbington brothers in a nearby cell. They admitted that Mother Gothel had told them about Rapunzel's hair and eventually double-crossed them.

Suddenly, the pub thugs from the Snuggly Duckling arrived and broke Flynn out of jail! They launched him over the prison walls and onto Maximus' back. Maximus had planned the entire escape! Flynn thanked him and, together, the heroes galloped off to rescue Rapunzel!

Back at the tower, Rapunzel sat in her bedroom, heartbroken. She held up the kingdom flag with the sun symbol and gazed at her wall of art. Then she noticed something amazing. She had been painting the sun symbol her whole life. She suddenly came to the realization that she was the lost princess!

Mother Gothel tried to justify her actions, but Rapunzel no longer believed her lies. Before Rapunzel could reach the window, Mother Gothel overpowered her.

Flynn finally arrived at the tower. "Rapunzel! Rapunzel, let down your hair!" he called.

Rapunzel's golden locks fell to the ground and Flynn began to climb. When he reached the top, he found Rapunzel chained in the middle of the room. He went to help her, but Mother Gothel wounded him with a dagger.

Rapunzel was desperate to save Flynn. She begged Mother Gothel to allow her to heal him. In return, Rapunzel promised Mother Gothel she would stay with her forever.

Mother Gothel agreed to the deal and unchained Rapunzel. She knew Rapunzel never broke a promise, but she chained Flynn to the wall to ensure he wouldn't follow them.

Rapunzel rushed to Flynn's side and placed her hair over his wound.

"No, Rapunzel, don't do this," begged Flynn.

"I'll be fine," said Rapunzel, looking into Flynn's eyes. "If you're okay, I'll be fine."

Flynn caressed her cheek. Then he suddenly reached for a shard of broken glass and cut off her hair! It instantly turned brown and lost its magic healing power.

"What have you done?!" Mother Gothel cried. Within moments she aged hundreds of years and turned to dust.

Rapunzel cradled Flynn in her arms and began to weep. A single golden tear fell upon Flynn's cheek. To Rapunzel's astonishment, the tear – and then Flynn's entire body – began to glow.

Flynn was healed. "Rapunzel!" he exclaimed.

The two embraced and shared their first kiss.

Flynn, Pascal and Maximus brought Rapunzel straight to the castle. Her parents rushed to hug her. They were filled with joy. Their daughter had finally been returned to them! Rapunzel felt her parents' love surround her as they all hugged each other tightly, a family once more.

Soon, all of the townspeople gathered for a welcome home party. The King and Queen were there, along with Flynn, Pascal, Maximus and the pub thugs. The people of the kingdom released floating lanterns into the sky. Their light had guided their princess home at last.